"Give all your worries to him,
because he cares for you."
1 Peter 5:7

The Standard Publishing Company, Cincinnati, Ohio
A division of Standex International Corporation
Text © 1994 by Kim Melanie Henry
Illustrations © 1994 by The Standard Publishing Company
All rights reserved.
Printed in the United States of America
01 00 99 98 97 96 95 94   5 4 3 2 1

Library of Congress Catalog Card Number 94-1122
ISBN 0-7847-0201-2
Cataloging-in-Publication data available
Designed by Coleen Davis

Scripture from the International Children's Bible, New Century Version,
© 1986, 1989 by Word Publishing, Dallas, Texas 75039.
Used by permission.

TWO PRAYERS
for PATCHES

By Kim Henry
Illustrated by Tim Bowers

LITTLE DEER
B·O·O·K·S
PSALM 42:1

Standard Publishing
Cincinnati, Ohio

Patches and Speckles
were playful puppies,
who never minded
a game or two.

They liked to ride in Harry's wagon,

splash in Harry's pool,

and play kick ball in the backyard.

Sometimes Patches and Speckles played by themselves, chasing squirrels into the woods.

Sometimes they got into mischief.

But they always came home
to sleep at the foot of Harry's bed.

**Then one fall night, Harry found Speckles
all by himself at the foot of the bed.**

Harry looked for Patches under the bed, in all the closets,

and behind the sofa. Patches was not in the house!

Harry and his father looked in the yard and in the woods, but Patches was not there.
They walked through the neighborhood calling, "Patches! Patches!" but they could not find the puppy anywhere.

"Maybe Patches needs to be by herself for a while,"
said Harry's mother.
"We will look for Patches again tomorrow,"
promised his father.

"Please keep Patches safe," prayed Harry
before he got into bed.

But in the morning, Patches was still missing. Harry and his mother made signs with a picture of Patches and the words "Missing Dog." They hung the signs on telephone poles up and down the streets of town. They hung signs at corners and in front of the school. They even asked Pete, who ran the grocery store, to hang a sign there.

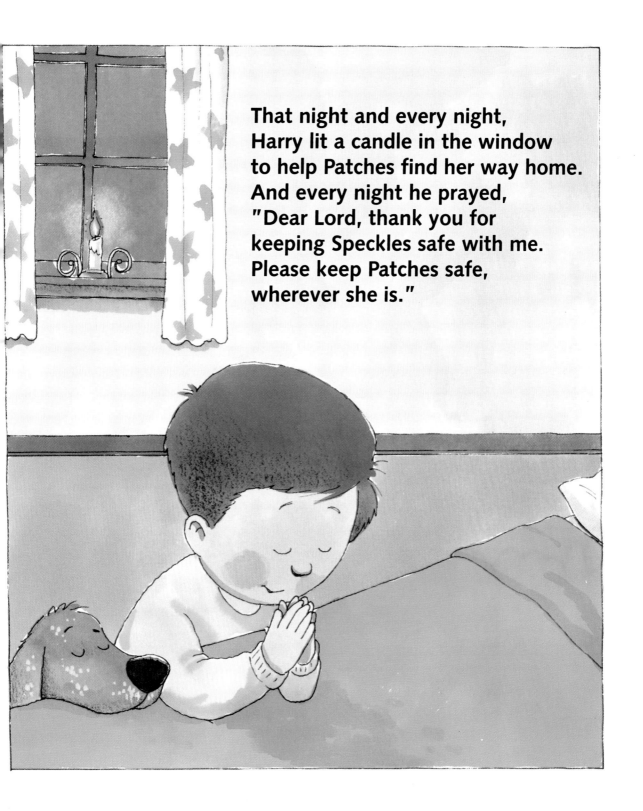

That night and every night,
Harry lit a candle in the window
to help Patches find her way home.
And every night he prayed,
"Dear Lord, thank you for
keeping Speckles safe with me.
Please keep Patches safe,
wherever she is."

And one night, while the candle was burning in Harry's window, Patches strayed into the library parking lot. She had followed the mail truck down many streets and rambled for days through many yards. She was hungry and thirsty.

Outside the library, a girl named Maggie was waiting for her mother to come. "Poor puppy," said Maggie. "I'll take you home and feed you. Maybe I can keep you."

But Maggie's mother shook her head
when she saw the puppy.

"You may bring the dog home, Maggie. But you must
try to find her owner."

Maggie fed Patches and
then watched her fall asleep
in a laundry basket full of
soft, warm towels.

"What will we name her?"
Maggie asked her mother.
"Remember, we can keep her
only for a short while,"
her mother said.

"I will call her
Maggie's-Dog-for-Now,"
said Maggie.

At first, Maggie's-Dog-for-Now was content just to eat and nap in the laundry basket. But as she got stronger, Maggie's-Dog-for-Now became very playful. She loved to chew on socks while Maggie sorted the laundry.

She rolled on the sofa,
leaving dog hair everywhere.

As time went on, Maggie's-Dog-for-Now got into more and more mischief. She loved to play in the mud.

She loved to chase Maggie's cat into highest tree.

And one day she ate four pork chops off the kitchen table.

"I love that dog, too, Maggie,"
said Maggie's mother.
"But you must find the owner."

Every day on her way home from school, Maggie looked for "Missing Dog" signs.
But the only signs she saw were faded and torn.

Maggie was discouraged.
"Somewhere, someone else loves you
even more than I do," she said,
holding the dog close.
"Please, Lord," prayed Maggie.
"Please help me find the owner of this dog."

The next day in the grocery store, Maggie and her mother told the cashier about their stray white dog with black patches. Pete heard them.
"That dog sounds like the dog Harry lost last fall," he said. "Her name was Patches."

That evening Maggie took Patches
to Harry's house.
A candle glowed in the window.
"I think you've been
greatly missed," she whispered
in the puppy's ear.

Maggie knocked on the door.
"Is this your dog?" she asked Harry
when the door opened.

But Maggie could tell by the look on his face
that she had come to the right place!